Participation Trophy
© 2018-2022 by Ira Rat
Art and Design by Ira Rat

This is a work of fiction. Names, characters, businesses, places, events, locales, and incidents are either the products of the author's imagination or used in a fictitious manner. Any resemblance to actual persons, living or dead, or actual events is purely coincidental

This book may not be reproduced in whole or in part, except for the inclusion of brief quotations in a review, without permission in writing from the author or publisher. No part of this publication may be reproduced, stored in or introduced into retrieval system, or transmitted, in any form, or by any means (electronic, mechanical, photocopying, recording, or otherwise), without prior permission of the publisher.

Requests for permission should be directed to filthylootpress@gmail.com

SPECIAL EDITION

Ira Rat's Participation Trophy

Filthy Loot

filthyloot.com

For Emily

Special thanks to: Amy M. Vaughn, Cody Goodfellow, Madison McSweeny, Luke Kondor, Garrett Cook, and Casey Jones.

John's Room

Kevin's dead.

The words were lit up in John's head like a "Game Over" screen, one that had not gone away in the passing weeks.

"Your brother is dead!" he would mumble to himself, while idly trying to find distraction that never came.

John's room looked like any typical middle American boy's room.

Well, except for the cement walls and sizeable eggshell-white washer and dryer that were continually going in the corner.

It hadn't been hard to convince his parents to let him take over the basement after Kevin's death.

Though when he thought about it, he couldn't really remember the conversation. Maybe he just moved down here and they had yet to notice.

Still, it was weird how, even now, with just the three of them, it was a never-ending avalanche of dirty clothes and Tide he had to deal with. If this was the price to pay for his autonomy, he thought, it was probably worth it. Not that his parents were around much these days; in fact, John couldn't remember the last time he had seen them.

Notes? Yes. Parents? It had been a while.

Well, notes and the dirty clothes.

His walls were covered in posters for The Clash, Ramones, and similar bands, bands he only vaguely cared about, having only inherited the decorations. The one thing he hadn't shared with his brother was his taste in music, but they made the walls look less like he was living in a prison cell.

Interspersed were posters for The Goonies, Indiana Jones, and other Spielbergesque adventure movies, aimed at his demographic, PG-13 (give or take a year or two). The kind of movies that could get a "shit" in here and there to excite the imagination, and just enough scantily clad girls to keep him interested.

From the cassette player came the jangly sound of Tom Petty. This, as well, wasn't the type of music he would have gone for personally, but it was what all the popular kids were listening to. So, fuck it, he had thought when he bought it from Walmart a couple of weeks ago.

Like most of his peers, he was just along for the ride. He tended to listen to whatever he noticed somebody else was wearing the t-shirt of, or what he saw on MTV. In the end, at least it was better than silence.

Like every afternoon, across from John on his

Star Wars sheets, Sam sat reading an old horror comic she found at a garage sale. The pages brown and brittle, he was surprised it wasn't falling apart in her hands. It had been something he wouldn't dare read; he couldn't even get through the edited-for-TV late-night horror show reruns that played on the UHF station.

Seeing Sam and John together, you would think they were brother and sister, maybe fraternal twins. They were both in their awkward teenage years—fourteen, to be exact.

John was a nerdy kid in the vein of Matthew Broderick, with an out-of-date shag haircut that could end up costing him teeth. His button-down shirt was a little too K-Mart to be smooth and didn't win him any "Best Looking" accolades.

Sam was the "girl" equivalent. Her short blond hair just touched the rims of her horn-rimmed glasses. The way she looked didn't get her picked on but kept her the sort of invisible that often made her feel like a ghost.

She couldn't quite get down the formula for "ladylike," at least that's what her mom enjoyed saying anytime she was within earshot. "Boys don't make passes at girls who wear glasses," her mom would say to her while pointing out how unfeminine she was. She would change the last words to fat asses, whenever Sam wanted seconds on dessert.

In her own estimation, Sam was a world away from the women she saw in music videos—she still wore the oversized t-shirts and cut-off jeans of her youth. It wasn't like she wasn't trying to look more mature.

Though her tough-guy act didn't help. She had spent more time in the principal's office than she could remember. If she could keep her smart mouth shut, maybe she would graduate sometime in this lifetime.

In John's room, they sat in their little worlds, just feet apart. John was the one who finally broke the silence when he jolted upright.

"Oh, hey, before I forget! I've got something to show you!"

Relieved that anything was going on, Sam dropped the comic to her side, trying not to look eager. Eager was the kiss of death.

On the comic's cover, a hand reached out from the dirt in front of a headstone. John caught a glimpse of it and shuddered.

Distracted, for a moment he thought about skipping what he was about to do and kissing her.

His hand went to his mouth and felt the hard steel of braces, quickly dispelling this thought. What if he cut Sam's lip with those things? She probably didn't even want him to anyway, right? She couldn't possibly want him to.

"I thought you'd gotten your 'doctor' phase, out of your system," she said as a mischievous grin spread over her face.

Caught off-guard, John looked at her for a few moments before he registered the joke. Sam was always joking; sometimes it was even harder to realize if she wasn't.

"Wha . . . huh? Oh, gross . . ." John knee-jerk protested before thinking too hard about it. "It's," suddenly he realized just how incredibly not-gross it would be. ". . . It's not that."

He got up and stuck his hand behind the headboard. From this mystery-hole, he pulled out a dusty leather book, a book that radiated, "Satanic Bible! Bring on the virgins!" On its black patchwork cover, the cryptic letters spelling out the title didn't look overtly evil, more like something on a "very special" episode of Geraldo. Though the book still gave off a menacing vibe that didn't scream, "$2.50

Head Shop Book of Magic," either.

"I found—" he paused, surprised by Sam's undivided attention. "I found this in Kevin's room. After . . ."

They sat, letting the moment build up between them. The two had already rehashed what had happened a million times over the past few weeks. She waved her hands in a gesture that clearly stated, let's skip the same conversation for now.

"What is it?" Sam asked.

"I dunno, I can't read it," John said.

Sam whipped her legs around on the bed and scooted over next to John in a crab walk. Planting herself cross-legged next to him, they both looked at the cover.

"I figured you took Latin," he tried to explain.

A look of pain crossed Sam's face before she

sighed and rolled her eyes at John. "Failed Latin, you mean."

John started to say something but couldn't come up with a rebuttal.

Sam sighed and took the book. She flipped through it as if trying to find the right page in a textbook. Quickly realizing she couldn't make heads or tails of any of it, she still made a good show of trying.

"Well, first of all, this isn't Latin . . ." she explained while continuing to flip through the pages. "I'm not even sure it is a language. It looks like Ozzy Osbourne's notebook."

John looked at her like she was speaking Latin.

"It looks like a prop from a metal video." She was satisfied with this analogy. "What do you think it is? Where did he get it? Kevin never seemed to be the headbanger type. Though, he did have a crush on

Siouxsie there for a moment," she continued in the faux seriousness of an expert. "Or was it one of the Banshees? No, it was one of the Go-Go's. I always get those two bands confused."

She laughed to herself, though John just stared at her like a dog watching a card trick. John's easy befuddlement was one of his more charming aspects. Sometimes it was so easy that it felt terrible.

John took the book from Sam, looking at the cover like a kid who dropped his ice cream cone. Here's where the strings should come in, Sam thought.

"Like I was saying," John started to say, "I found it in his room after . . ."

Sam turned her head away and strained with every mind-controlling muscle in her body to stop the compulsive monologue about his brother.

He stopped, it worked!

Participation Trophy

"I found it in his room, buried under some other weird stuff."

John omitted a little as he told her about sneaking into his brother's room. He headed straight for a hidden loose floorboard under Kevin's bed. There sat Kevin's treasure—a stack of Hustler magazines and a considerable baggie of marijuana. He had been worried that there would only be firecrackers from the year before. This had been a surprise. The pot went in his front pocket and the Hustlers under his arm. Underneath them was the book. Thinking it might also be something his parents would get upset about if they ever found, he grabbed the remaining ill-gotten loot and scurried back to his room.

"Yeah, you know, just weird . . . stuff. Well, this, I found this . . . It's weird, you know?"

Sam looked from the book to John suspiciously. Her visions of teenage treasure varied drastically from what had been in there.

She relented. "Do you think it has anything to do . . ."

"Again, I dunno. It's not like we'd been talking that much since Kevin broke up wi—"

Fuck fuck fuckity fuck fuck, she thought, here it goes . . .

Sadly, she had heard the story too many times in the last few weeks. Boy meets girl, boy falls in love with girl, boy and girl date for the first few years of high school, then girl spreads her legs for the entire football team after homecoming . . . and boy loses his shit.

She felt terrible that her inner monologue sounded so bored, but there was only so much one could take.

"I just thought, maybe . . ." John continued like an orphaned child asking for another bowl of soup. His lip quivered a little bit like he was about to cry. Sam often found herself staring at his lips in moments of proximity like this.

"Alright, alright, alright. Let me take another look at this sucker." She couldn't stand to see a boy cry. She removed her glasses, wiped them on her shirt, and guiltily took the book back from John.

Flipping through it once again, she noticed that it was handwritten and illustrated in blood-red ink. Interesting choice, she thought. The illustrations made her horror comics look like Bambi. For a moment, she lingered on an image of a comically large penis with a knife splaying it down the middle. Disney, this was not.

As she tried to read it, John watched her eyes begin to flicker back up in her head. From inside the basement, a wind started blowing. After looking around, he realized it was coming from the book itself. From behind her, an unhealthy lime-green glow lit up like a witch like a witch in one of her comics.

In her head, she was no longer in the basement. She was elsewhere, watching the book pass from hand to hand through untold years. Involuntarily, Sam started chanting, The words came out cold and emotionless, as if they were coming from a different world, hidden somewhere deep inside her chest. As the chant churned in her mouth, a deep rumbling sound came moistly from within, a gray pool of malice.

John wanted . . . no, he needed his mommy! Before he could cry out for her, a gale-force wind blew the book shut with the weight and finality of the door to a crypt.

Sam looked to John with that same cat-like grin

she had given him five-million times before, but with a small trickle of something blue-green oozing out of the corner of her mouth. She quickly wiped it away with the back of her hand.

"Just messin' with you," she said. John noticed that the smile stopped just short of her eyes. They were cold and ruthless, like she could eat him alive. "I have no idea what the fuck it says."

John sat and stared.

"Sooooo. . . wanna go grab some pizza?"

Kelly-Green Lawns & Cheese Pizza

Synchronized lawn sprinklers shot jets of cold, crisp, fluoridated water, just missing the pair by an inch or two—though little droplets collected on their shoulders.

John and Sam walked down their painfully ordinary suburban street. A street straight out of a Norman Rockwell painting. House after house, white picket fences and red doors lay beyond perfectly manicured kelly-green lawns.

As they strolled down the sprawl, they passed a jock and a cheerleader—wholesome, Leave It to Beaver kids—making out against a tree. The all-star athlete fondled the breasts of his conquest causing Sam to look down at her own, which lay hidden under the Tasmanian Devil t-shirt she'd worn weekly since third grade.

I guess there's nothing sexy about Looney Tunes, she thought.

John appeared to be over whatever spooked him so badly about her joke in the basement. Still, Sam kept an eye on him as they lingered to witness sport-o's hand disappear under the thin elastic of the cheerleader's skirt.

If his hand were any deeper, he'd probably lose it, along at any scholarships, she thought. Looking back down, Sam noted her cutoffs and shook her head.

She thought for a second that maybe she should ask them, John included, if they should get a room. At least two of them might enjoy that. Though if she opened her mouth, John would probably end up with a few fresh bruises.

Monsters with human faces.

Sam's attention waned as she saw that the nearby lamppost was covered in flyers. Each one had a picture of a pimple-faced geek, most of them wearing coke-bottle glasses, their hair a wet mat on their forehead. All of them bearing the caption, Have You Seen Me?

She would have made a joke about them if it didn't bother her that they looked like her and John.

For a second, it made her uncomfortable that all the geeks seemed to be running away from home. Or worse yet, getting snatched by some perv who had a thing for geeks.

They walked on.

As they neared the train tracks, Sam and John came across some goth kids. They were dressed all in black and puffing away at their clove cigarettes. Sam pictured herself dressed like that. She was sure her mother would kill her. The goths looked like the kids on the posters. Though, with the addition of twelve layers of pancake makeup and a gallon of kohl eyeliner, each.

To Sam, this fact didn't mean much considering that most of the misfits in their town had two options: if you didn't want to look like a dork, your only other choice was Robert Smith.

As they passed by the funeral procession in home-made band shirts, an unmistakable look of distaste crossed John's face. Sam remembered the time John asked out a girl in a The Damned shirt, only to get mocked and laughed at by her gaggle of ankh-wearers.

After what seemed like an eternity in the weary October sun, Sam and John reached the railroad tracks. Its concrete embankments were covered in small-town graffiti: "EB + EH" in a heart, heavy metal band names, pentagrams, upside-down crosses. Some of them even looked like the runes in the book.

John stopped short as he read, "Helen loves head." Sam pictured him going through a mile-long list of the girls he knew, checking to see if he knew a Helen. From the looks of it, he had trouble putting a face to the name.

When they finally got through the door of Joe's Pizza, they stepped up and ordered their slices at the bar. Their presence was conspicuous among the daytime drunks. The Joe's had opened in the early '70s and had never remodeled. It had red plastic everything, including the cups and the gaudy vinyl booth benches.

Wompa wompa wompa, the sound of the Ms. Pac-Man machine echoed from a dark corner. Everything was cast in high shadow by the green fixtures over each booth. The third one was theirs and was where John and Sam resumed their game of silence.

Losing this round, Sam started. "I'm sorry, okay? I was trying to make you smile!" She reached out and grabbed his chin and smooshed his cheeks together, mimicking something she once saw his grandma do when he was too old for such affection.

"You know I love the way you smile at me, baby. Give me some of those high beams!"

They both smiled despite themselves. It was moments like this when Sam saw the old John and remembered how desperately she wanted him back.

Again, she found herself staring at his lips. This time they were abstracted to the maw of a sea creature. Just add a couple of tentacles and she would have been pulled right in there, like the heroine in an underwater adventure.

John looked uncomfortably and slightly sad, enough so that she let go of his face. His cheeks were candied red, but she couldn't tell if it was from her fingers or embarrassment.

"This isn't like the time that you convinced me that Bev was in love with me," he grumbled. "Remember when you were controlling the thingy on the Ouija board that night?" Clearly annoyed, he pulled a card from deep within his deck of petty grievances.

Sam sat up defensively. "Oh no! Beverly is totally in love with you . . ." Trailing off, she slumped back, the groan of the vinyl seat protested her movement. "It's gross." Her final words came out like a puff of smoke.

John's face caved in. "What's gross about her?"

Fiddling with her straw, Sam answered,

"Nothing . . . I suppose." And then to herself, "Anyway, I said it was gross."

The waitress showed up with their slices.

She was the wrong side of thirty, just beyond pleasantly plump and forced to wear a cigarette girl uniform that was at least two sizes too small.

Despite all of this, she held to her dogeared paperback copy of Dianetics and was overly sweet to them, even though she knew she wasn't getting tipped.

"Can I get you two sweethearts—" she started. A softly diffused redness spread all the way out to Sam's earlobes. "—some refills? Coke?"

They nodded in unison. "I'll just be a sec!"

John played with the parmesan that he had laid nearly an inch thick on top of his slice, making little snow paths with his finger. A painful amount of time went by as they eased back into their game.

The silence was so thick that John could have been making little paths through it rather than the grated cheese.

This time John lost, resigned but embarrassed by all the thoughts swimming around his head. "Anyway, it's not like I'm supposed to be Mr. Happy—"

Sam couldn't help herself. She snorted loudly and whispered, "Mr. Happy, ha-ha."

Unfazed, John continued. He was used to this type of behavior by now. She didn't do it on purpose, at least he didn't think so. "—Go-Lucky, right about now. You know, right after you see your brother with his head blown—"

"—right off my shoulders if it wasn't attached," the server said as she swooped in. "Two Cokes!" She bent over and placed the drinks on their coasters.

As her massive cleavage dropped down to

eye-level, John noted the server's nametag: "Helen." Instinctively, his reflex was to feel mildly grossed-out, but maybe not as disgusted as he should be.

Several more moments passed before Sam sighed.

"Well, why are you mad at me about it?" she asked. "It's not like I had anything to do with it. We're the innocent ones here. Sarah did sleep with—"

"—The whole football team is coming in for a pre-game celebration." The server swooped in again. "Would you kiddos mind moving over to the bar?"

Sheet-white, John looked to Sam for support, cold impotence grabbing him by his developing manhood.

"I," he stuttered, "I think it's time to go, anyway." John reached into his pocket and quickly palmed a dollar in nickels and dimes for a tip. The biggest he ever left in his life.

He and Sam guzzled their Cokes, knowing that a room full of football team wasn't a good place for them to be.

John gave Helen a last once-over, lingering on her bountiful ass, as he dropped the change on the table with a conspicuous clatter.

The "J" Stands For Nothing

Sam sat alone in an empty classroom. She was doodling in her unicorn Trapper Keeper, in the amateurishly ornate style that you would only find in such a three-ring plastic binder. By all outward appearances, she had the intense look of somebody who's cramming for a test.

On the page she has written:

"Mrs. Fox
Mrs. Michael Fox
Mrs. Michael J. Fox
Mrs. J. Fox"

Just below a whisper, she asked herself, "I wonder what the J stands for . . . Jared? Jethro? John?"

She then switched the color on her multi-colored pen and moved to the opposite page.

Her earnest expression turned somewhat hazy. As the pen came back up from the nosedive of the bottom of the heart, her eyes flickered back. Rolling, so that only the whites shown.

"John + Sam"

John walked in, waking Sam up from her glassy-eyed hypnosis. Not wanting to get caught in the act, she threw her hand over the drawing. He sat down and acted as if she was not obviously hiding something.

"That's stupid!" he mumbled to her.

Her response was a confused look, so he continued. "The J doesn't stand for anything. Why would you take it?" He pointed to the tiny visible corner of the previous page. "Anyway, his career has been kind of shaky, other than Teen Wolf, that is."

Participation Trophy

"Oh, yeah, you're right!" Sam sighed with relief.

Closing the Trapper Keeper, she saw that she had drawn a cheerleader with pigtails. The caricature's' unnaturally blonde decapitated head impaled on a megaphone sticking from the wet end, all the way out through the top between her hair ties.

"So, what do you want to do tonight?" John asked, more out of habit than actually wanting to know. They were probably going to go to his house and sit silently in the oddly domestic situation they had grown into.

It's all fun and games until your brother blows his brains out, John thought to himself. In his head, he saw his brother in his room, the way that he had found him: mouth-to-barrel, the record still spinning on the turntable. Joy Division, fucking Joy Division. The image was stuck on instant replay, over and over.

Mr. Bartleby walked into the classroom. Their teacher, a bearded man somewhere between the ages of forty and Methuselah, wore a D.A.R.E. t-shirt and jeans. His ponytail and earring denoted just how hard he was trying to win over his students.

His ungodly wholesomeness, though, was a dead giveaway. He had to be a sham. Sam had seen a short segment on TV about a guy in Chicago who had dozens of teenagers buried in his crawl space. Chicago wasn't too far away. She wondered how many bodies were in Bartleby's basement.

"Time for class, team," he started, looking at nobody in particular, though his big smile advertised just how happy he was to be there.

What a fake, Sam thought.

"If you've been asking yourself, For heaven's sake, Teach, we're not done with the unit on Drug Prevention yet, right? We haven't learned all that we need to know to keep us away from dancing with

Mr. Brownstone! Or his sister Mary Jane!'" Bartleby hammed. "Well, you can ask my good friend Nancy what the answer to that is!"

Bartleby's smile wavered for a moment. Waiting in front of the class for an uncomfortably long time wasn't anything new. Still, he wasn't entirely sure that it encouraged audience participation. If not for his breathing, it looked like someone had paused reality.

Crestfallen that another one of his jokes had fallen on deaf ears, he continued. "'No,' kids. The answer is 'N.O.' Just like what you should be saying when people offer you drugs and alcohol! Or, for that matter, when even your best friend offers you something even worse."

Not for the first time, the kids sat in confused silence, who were still paying attention anyway. The majority of them had already tuned him out for the period and a sizable chunk were so high their eyes burned red from across the room.

Ira Rat

One of the red-eyes chuckled like he heard something funny, but he already couldn't remember what.

"As all of you will remember from watching my interview last night on Heather Lock's show . . ." More silence as he waited for the kids to shower him with admiration for being interviewed by a local cable access talk-show host none of them had heard of. "What we were talking about, gang, is the biggest gateway drug in America right now. It isn't reefer, it isn't coke or even 'ludes. It's the dark prince himself! Lucifer. The Devil, coming packaged in your Led Zeppelin metal albums and your Pac-Man-fever comic books!"

From the front row, one of the better students tried to remind him that this was, in fact, a public school.

"That's right, Tim. This is a public school, so you don't know who all is out there! And Satan is a public menace! All I'm saying is this prince isn't hip, and he's not 'with-it.' He's not even going to give you any Purple Rain." The dramatic pause he took felt a little needy.

"Though he will let you go crazy!" Bartleby stopped because, in his mind, there would be a big laugh and outpouring of emotion right here. These kids today, they gave him nothing.

Undeterred, he continued, "He's not cool, he's just trying to take you down the path of addiction, prostitution, violation, and damnation! Here, now, pass these back," he said, finally giving up on winning the students over. Today at least. There was always tomorrow and the next day and . . .

To the front row, he started tossing out stacks of poorly drawn, generic Chick-tract style mini-comic books entitled (L)ucifer, (S)atanism & (D)amnation.

They almost looked like he made them himself on the school's Xerox machine. It wouldn't surprise Sam if she opened it and saw his name on the byline.

"Now, students, this will be a quick read. I want you to go over it and then use the rest of the period to write a 1,000-word essay on why the devil . . ." His voice started to get drowned out by the sound of the kids pushing back their chairs to get their backpacks so they could do the assignment.

Knock, Knock

Troy's door was closed.

This made his mom nervous, more nervous than her average background level of anxiety that hid safely behind the frosted glass of her breakfast Valium.

"Knock, knock," she fussed, giving the door a tap with her aquamarine Lee Press-On nails.

"It's supper time!" She tried in vain to feign casualness, but her nerves betrayed her, pitching her voice in a hiccup.

From experience, she knew better than to just come barging into a boy's room. Especially a teen boy's room. She didn't want a repeat of what happened last winter. She hadn't been able to look at Troy's brother, or that cute little My Buddy doll, the same way since.

It was bad enough when "the boys" were in the bathroom for hours on end. It had gotten so the sound of running water tied her stomach knots.

Despite her best efforts to the contrary, "Mom" did have some idea of the goings-on behind closed doors. She had older brothers, and the things she saw, she didn't even dare tell her shrink.

Instead, she chose to coyly exchange pleasantries at $50 an hour.

"Troy! Honey! I know you're in there! For goodness sake! Homemade pizza! Cheese! It's your favor—"

"Harder!" moaned a woman's voice from inside the room.

Participation Trophy

Before his mom could process this, the door unlatched itself and opened silently.

The room was dark.

Entering, she didn't notice Troy's stillness, or the belt pulled snugly around his neck. Details she would recall vividly to the police reporter passed right by her as she floated through his room, dodging dirty clothes and moldering dishes.

What she did notice was a large group of people having sex on her son's TV. The unbridled lust of the scene she was witnessing was enough to make the devil blush, not that you would notice with his red cheeks and all. This small "joke" made her smirk despite her fury. Then again, she also had to be kept from laughing at funerals.

Mesmerized by the debauchery of the orgy on the screen, she barely noticed as she reached out to touch Troy's shoulder.

The chair turned.

The Fires of Hell

Sam and John walked next to the train tracks. John was smoking—he'd never smoked before. Cutting short in front of John, Sam confronted him with a devilish grin.

"I can see the fires of hell burning in your cherry there, young man! Are you willing to let the fallen one suck out your soul through your Mr. Happy for the rich, fulfilling flavor of Marlboro Country?" Her fire and brimstone act complete, she grabbed the cigarette, dropped to her knees, and mocked fellatio with the butt between her lips.

She wasn't a smoker, so she began to cough. The sight of both her smoking and bluntly sexual pantomime made John feel awkward.

"F that!" came John's response. The

self-censorship was corny, even for him. Pinching the cigarette from her mouth, he once again started smoking but didn't inhale, having just picked up the habit.

Sam feigned the shock and horror of a southern belle, but was already giggling. She withered to the ground. "Do you kiss your daddy with that mouth?"

She actually liked seeing him smoking. It made him look brat-packy, in a good way.

"No, but your mother doesn't seem to mind . . . much." John's quick-witted response was entirely unexpected, even by him. He stuttered out a little cough. Sam looked at him, vexed. She should have known better than to have opened herself up like that.

Her free association was getting the best of her: the term opening herself up, she pictured Sarah, Kevin's girlfriend, wrapping her legs around one letterman jacket-clad hunk after another. Full of hatred, she quickly dispelled the image from her mind, but not before Sarah's face was mentally airbrushed over with her own.

"Anyway, it doesn't even matter," John continued. "There aren't any devils. There aren't demons and ghosts yelling out, 'I'll eat your soul, I'll eat your soul!'"

Sam smiled a little to herself, remembering the horror movie that they had tried to watch the year before on Halloween, before being busted by John's mom. She had known John wasn't going to make it through the first twenty minutes, anyway. Why'd he have to scare so easy?

"Or any of that Sunday-school bullshit. There's just this and nothingness." John finished the cigarette and flicked it in the direction of nowhere like he was James Dean.

"So, you think there's no point to life, and after that, it's just the big black? What about Kevin?" She looked at him, the most earnest she'd been in ages.

"Just dirt in the ground." John caught himself for a moment. "Errr . . . I mean mantelpiece . . . in his case. I guess."

This wasn't the time to make any unnecessary digs so Sam didn't point out the weirdness of this statement.

"Does that still bug you out?" she asked, quickly burying her unresolved feelings. Kevin's absence had left a hole in both of their lives. Who knew that one bullet could mortally wound three people?

"Not as much, I guess. I notice it about as much as I notice all my participation trophies." He stopped and fished another cigarette out of the front pocket of his button-up. "I guess that's all his urn is."

Participation Trophy

Lighting up dramatically, he took a drag that found its way to his lungs and coughed, "Just a participation trophy." Looking into the distance, he spat out a little piece of nothing on the tip of his tongue.

"De-Yark. Have you been listening to that geeoth stuff again? Love, love will tear us . . ." Taking shelter by trying to find some happiness again, Sam started belting the song out in a faux-baritone.

In John's head was the image of Kevin sitting in his room alone, looking down at the revolver in his hand; the gun that he found in his parent's bedroom one day when he and John were wasting time looking for their dad's pornos. In his other hand was a picture of Sarah. Low in the background, Joy Division played.

"Apart aga-yannnnn," Sam vamped like a Vegas-era version of Ian Curtis, complete with knee-drop and imaginary cape fanned out like Batman.

The daggers shooting out of John's eyes were hard to ignore, so she cut herself off before another round of the chorus.

John's eyes mellowed.

"Sorry, you know I hate that pretentious goth bullshit. They're a bunch of posers. Anyway, when you sing like that it makes me feel weird, like I'm hanging out with a dude."

Sam looked away. It was the first time she'd ever been referred to as "a dude," though his lack of desire for her to be one seemed a little promising.

"But your mother loves my beautiful voice!" Sam continued in her baritone, not missing an opportunity to get a jab in.

"Well, go sing for her, why don't you?" he countered, pulling yet another mouthful of smoke.

"Oh, trust me," she shot back, "when we're together, we siiiiiiiiiiiiiing!"

The daggers returned. Sam won. She always won. Eventually, at least. John thought back to all the times she had gotten the better of him—too many times to count. Like most things, he quickly let this go; after all, it was Sam he was thinking this about. What would he do without Sam? She was as inevitable as needing oxygen . . . or missing his brother.

A voice in his head told him it was time to change the subject. "Want to see what else I found in my brother's drawer?" He flicked his cigarette in the same direction as the last.

After a moment or two of fishing in his pocket,

he produced a poorly-rolled joint, no thicker than a toothpick. Never having seen one before, but knowing what this meant, Sam did a cartoon double-take before slipping into her best Gene Wilder impression.

"Are the fires of hell a-glowin?"

Cheated

The skunky smell of pot, sweet and musky, was on his lips as they pressed against hers. She closed her eyes. As they kissed, John's hands began to play a little rough on her body. Grabbing, rather than touching, all the places she had wanted him to be gentle.

When she opened her eyes, John was no longer there. Instead, a jock dropped in his place. His hard hands felt good until they didn't anymore.

The third hand on her shoulder, Sam knew, was Sarah's. In a whisper, Sarah told her what she had to do to get John back again. The knife she placed in Sam's hand didn't leave room for subtle interpretation.

It felt heavy.

Blood poured out of the jock's stomach as the life faded from his eyes.

Waking up before John's return, Sam felt a little cheated. The slutbag had taken something else away from her.

The Weekend

John sat alone in his room not watching the music videos that played loudly on his TV. Instead he flipped intently through one of the magazines he found in his brother's room. A faint fog of pot smoke could still be seen in the air as he zoned off in his little pornographic world.

The basement door slammed, and Sam came flying down the stairs. Despite his visible impairment, John was quick enough to hide the evidence of his masturbatory studying under his pillow.

"Did you hear?" Out of breath, Sam nearly yelled at him when she got to the foot of his bed. In his haze, John took a second to decipher if this was real or another fantasy. He'd had some like this before, but not about Sam. Well, not often with her in a starring role.

As she stood over him, clothes not coming off, he realized that this wasn't a dream. Slightly disappointed, he tried to sharpen his focus.

"What about your . . ." John trailed off, unable to come up with a joke fast enough due to his dulled responses.

"Kevin's dead!" she said, her eyes grey-blue moons swimming on the tightening baby fat of her face. Suddenly he was lost in her mouth, unable to swim to . . . Wait what did she say?

John sat up taller, suddenly sharper from the thought that she was yanking his chain. The cruelty of his joke was beyond anything he ever thought she was capable of. **"Yeah, I know my bro—"**

"No, dumbfuck, not your brother. ALL-STATE Kevin, most-likely-to-succeed

Participation Trophy

Kevin! Whatchamacallit football thingy Kevin!" Her excitement could have been viewed as giddiness if he didn't know her any better.

She loved breaking news, especially anything that was out of the ordinary for their dull suburban lives. "Oh yeah, and Steve Bell ran away from home. Surprise, surprise. Another geek goes AWOL."

John couldn't picture this Kevin #2 but shook his head no. The word "football" brought up the faces of roughly a dozen kids, but they all looked the same to him.

As for Steve, he was drawing a blank there, too. He just assumed he wore thick glasses and had bad acne; that was the type that had been disappearing around here of late. He wondered if they were all going Mazes and Monsters, running around the sewers looking for a Hobbit ring.

"Well, it seems like this Kevin was out partying with all the other jock-os when everyone else went to go skinny-dipping, and he stayed behind to watch the fire. Maybe he was watching it a little too closely . . . because he fell headfirst into it." One hand, representing fire, slapped the other that was probably meant to be the all-stater's head. Composing herself, she continued: "They found him barbecued an hour or so after they'd been playing pin-the-cock-in-the-cheerleader with the Tiffanies."

"The Tiffanies" was a term that always kind of annoyed John. It took someone who's dismissed so often to find sympathy for people so lacking in the ability to be empathized with. He knew that Sam's act was all show. "They're not all named . . ."

Looking more hurt than she had the right to be, she said, "Yeah, one's name was Sarah, and unfortunately, she wasn't helping ol' Kev tend to the fire." Her eyes burned at the thought of the other girl.

"What do you have against her anyway? You're always poking at her. It's not her fau—"

Participation Trophy

"It's not her fault? Did she trip and land squarely on the pricks of the entire football team? It's a wonder they haven't all gotten herpes."

"Agh . . .she doesn't have herp—" John began raising his voice in defense of his brother's long-time girlfriend, the girl he thought one day might be his sister.

A sister he had pleasured himself to thoughts of too many times to count, but a sister nonetheless.

"And how would you know? You don't owe that c-bag anything. You know what happened just as well as I do." Sam remembered Sarah telling her what she should do to the jock in her dream.

"She didn't do anything, he did. It was his choice. Anyway, I'm not defending her. I'm just not going to run her out of town with pitchforks the way that you and the rest of the school are willing to. I've known her almost as long as I've known you.

"We only know the rumors. We don't even know Sarah's side of the story. We don't know what was going through either one of their heads when these things were happening. It's not like we have a crystal ball to go back and ask Kevin why he would do such a stupid fucking thing. Who knows? It could have been a test he failed. What if he was unhappy with the way he tied his shoes that morning? It's not exactly like he was Mr. Chipper there at the end.

"We never even heard the rumor about what she did until after the funeral. What if Kevin hadn't ever even heard anything about it? People commit suicide every day. This time it just happened to be my brother." The after-school-special monologue took it out of him.

That cut it. In Sam's mind, John was either on her side or the whore's. "Never mind then." Noticing the dirty magazine half-hidden under his pillow and the minor fog of smoke, it was clear that she wasn't going to win him over through argument. "It doesn't matter. It looks like you're busy anyway!"

Sam stomped back up the steps. The sound of his door slamming shut was like a cannon blast echoing through his cement room. Confused by her parting words, he quickly forgot all the nonsense lodged in his head and relaxed back into his haze. Knowing his priorities, he pulled the magazine out and started flipping through it again.

The "College Babes of '84" patiently awaited his return from the other side of the glossy paper.

Morning Announcements

Mr. Bartleby stood looking at the classroom speaker as if the source of the voice droning from it was God, Himself.

His D.A.R.E. shirt looked a little worse for wear, as if he hadn't taken it off since last week. All the students thought he lived in his car and parked it down by the river. The jocks had spread the rumor one night when his presence there had ruined one of their parties. Nobody knew where he really lived.

The principal continued, "For those of you in attendance, the funeral services for Kevin and Troy will be this Friday. Unexcused absences will be spending next Saturday in detention. No excuse for unexcused absences.

Participation Trophy

"Also, the parents of both Eric Spellman and Steve Bell are still looking for information regarding their whereabouts. Steve Bell was last seen after chess club last Friday. If you have any information, either come to the office or call the police department at . . ."

John wondered to himself why the jocks were only called by their first names, while the geeks he had to call by both their first and last names.

Bartleby shook his head. "See what the trappings of the flesh will get you? Partying, porno, and too much Pong will get you every time."

From the back row, one of the red-eyed kids asked if that would be on the test. The students sat in silence, not knowing if it was a real question or not. Shaking his head, Bartleby confirmed that it wouldn't be.

"Though it might not not be on the test, either," he smiled and teased solemnly.

Sam and John looked at each other distantly, normally this kind of weirdness would have brought both of them a decent laugh, but not today.

Sam didn't look all that different, but she was not quite the same as the day before. Her hair was a little more "done" than usual, the lip gloss was new to the package as well, and maybe she was even wearing a little make-up, too? Or was it that she appeared to be a little paler than usual?

There had been a virus going around the school.

John's clothes smelled like a Grateful Dead concert, but nobody was paying close enough attention to notice. In his notebook, he had "Helen Loves Head" written out in stiff, clumsy, boy writing.

To say that his mind was elsewhere would be an understatement. As the Oedipal excess of his masturbation fantasy filled his thoughts, he gazed off into nothing at all.

Sam's Room

As visually busy as John's room was, with all its posters and weird paraphernalia, Sam's was not—just four white walls, a bed with a not-quite-girlie pink bedspread, and a desk with only a cup of pencils on it. Her family wasn't exactly from the other side of the tracks, but they were track-adjacent.

In the corner, her Rainbow Brite night light was the latest soldier of the night watch. A watch that had been guarding her against the creatures under her bed since she was born.

In her head, her hand was John's hand touching her in the places she wanted John to kiss her. In her mind, she saw his lips and the three stupid hairs that it had taken him months to grow. In her head, they were in an abandoned house. She didn't know how she had come up with that scenario, but it seemed to fit this fantasy.

He stopped touching her and pulled out the book. Not this shit again, she thought as the fantasy derailed. "Fucking no!" she internally screamed as he asked her once again to read from the book. Could she help him? He didn't know how to read the goddamn book. Why does she have to be the one to read it? Over and over, that blood-red scrawl, spidery and obtuse.

She doesn't fucking know what it says, could they please go back to what they were doing? She had brought along the nurse's outfit and everything! "I don't want to read your stupid fucking book!" she yelled at him. His lips began to pout, and her resolve withered. One more time from the top, she thought.

Cheese Pizza

A morbidly obese, balding man in a white shirt and apron brought them their pizza. It was the owner, Joe. From the look on his face, John was disappointed by today's substitute server.

Joe was a nice enough guy . . . wait, no he wasn't. Sweat sprayed off him like a garden sprinkler. He plopped down the paper plates on the table with, "There you go, two slices of cheese!" And he lingered, looking at Sam a little too long.

If she wasn't purposefully ignoring everyone, trying to get under John's skin, she might have gotten up and left due to the sheer perviness of his gaze. Joe's eyes settled on her top, which was cut just low enough to be dangerous. The apparent change in the dynamics of his jeans would have make her skin crawl, if she had noticed.

When Sam looked toward John, Joe decided it was time to get out of there.

"So . . . you skipping?" Sam perked up as she asked, knowing the answer, but hoping for the miracle of John not being a scaredy-cat. When it came to school, he never broke the rules.

"Why would I go to the funeral? I didn't know or like him. So, I might as well go to class."

She looked at him like he missed the point.

"Are you talking about skipping class? Fuck no, fuck that! Why would I do that?" John gave Sam the same suspicious glare he'd give someone who had just asked him if he ever thought about pulling a bank heist.

"I dunno, I thought maybe we could go somewhere and hang out, you know, like old times. We could do fun shit like we used to. These days it's like, if we're not arguing, we're talking about your brother, and neither one of those activities is doing either one of us much good, are they?" In the back of her mind, she felt like she had heard her mother use most of the same argument on her father on more than a few occasions.

"And risk detention? Count me out," he said. Then, shaking parmesan onto his pizza, he added, "Anyway, you're making it sound like we're an old married couple."

Sam gave John a playful look. "Wuss."

John's ego was bruised but he wasn't budging. "A wuss that won't have to go to detention on a Saturday."

"Whatevs, Becky." Sam faintly smelled John's dirty-hippy funk and wondered if he was still smoking without her. She had enjoyed the day by the tracks, but they hadn't done that since.

Participation Trophy

The skunky smell of pot, sweet and musky, was on the lips—the lips that she had been so often fixated on—that pressed against hers. As they kissed, no wait . . . that was a dream. Wasn't it? She couldn't remember.

"What, you want detention?" The stick up John's ass was nearly visible from where Sam sat. She thought potheads were supposed to be easy going.

"C'mon, it's not like they're even going to notice. Most of the school is going to be there. It's like prom, but without the Tiffianies giving blowies to all the lettermen. Well . . . hopefully not. I just thought we could go do something fun together. Come on!"

John sighed, he had just about enough of this. "Like what?"

Sam laughed a little to herself and half mumbled, "Doctor?"

The Principal's Office

The principal was on the intercom talking about how Jake Haas was missing, and about how Tim the something-or-another's head had been found in the woods, but his body was still missing. All the while Bartleby interjected his own theories about what was really going on around here.

"These kids that keep disappearing are being pulled off into satanic cults—being shipped nationwide to perform their 'services' for bank owners and politicians." Bartleby went on. He had read the newspapers. It was happening all over. "There isn't a town nationwide that don't have at least one cult killing pets and running international sex rings."

Participation Trophy

Sam and John sat in their seats, watching his melt-down.

"What is going on around here?" John asked. "People are dropping off like flies."

"It's only a few," Sam replied, "and a few missing dweebs, not that anybody is saying much about them. We'll still have enough jocks and geeks to make it to prom." John gave her a look like he wasn't following her thread of conversation.

"What?" she continued. "There are a gazillion popular kids in this school, and more than enough of the others to go around. We can lose a few. The team won't be hurting for a while."

Sam's hair was curlier, maybe even somehow a little longer, dress pants had replaced her jeans, and she was definitely wearing make-up; it didn't look too bad on her. She sat there talking like a teenage Nazi, and he was checking her out . . .

He cut himself off.

This is Sam he was thinking about. They took baths together as children, for god's sake. It wasn't the first time he'd felt this way, but come on man. He had to pull it together. It wasn't like she thought of him that way, anyway. Right?

The self-doubt that stirred in his stomach was enough for him to doubt his sanity most days, let alone believe even Sam could like him. Not in that way, at least.

"In a week we'll already have lost, like, a quarter of the entire team. It's not exactly like we're going to Lincoln." He feebly defended his anti-death stance, while in his mind, he was still trying to figure out exactly what was different about Sam.

"Why does it matter how many we have on the team? We can always send in the water boy." Sam laughed to herself, picturing Trevor the water boy going in and immediately being pulled out on a stretcher.

John looked down at the reading they were supposed to be working on, about how the devil wants to give you heroin. "Honestly, I dunno. I'm surprised I even knew how many people were on the team."

"That's what she said," Sam interjected impishly.

John looked confused, then a little hurt. He had the face of someone who wished they could go one day without having to think about arguably the most significant day of their life.

Besides that, he was tired of defending Sarah to Sam. It's not like it should even be his job. She wasn't his girlfriend, but he didn't want to see anybody getting bullied, even behind their back, even Sarah.

"So . . . about the book." Sam sensed the need for a subject change, so she interjected a topic that had been weighing on her mind.

John gave her a look like he hadn't thought of the book in weeks, because he hadn't.

"The book from your brother's—" Sam continued.

"Yeah, what about it?" The tin-foil trap of his mind weakly snapped at the subject matter.

"Well, did you figure it out?" she asked, knowing full well that he hadn't even thought about it.

"It's been two weeks. Not only am I not smart enough to figure out what it says, but things have also been a little busy." John was edgy, not wanting to answer questions about what he'd been doing. "With all that's been going on the last few days, I mean."

"The dead kids? You didn't even like any them, and they sure didn't give a fuck about you!" Her voice jumped up at the end, catching Bartleby's attention.

Participation Trophy

If there was one thing you weren't going to get away within his classroom, it was dropping the Hail Mary of curses. Well that, or taking the Lord's name in vain, but that was beside the point.

"SAMANTHA! Principal's office, pronto!"

Poe, formerly Nathan before he discovered The Sisters of Mercy, sat in the principal's outer office. Dressed from head to toe in thrift-store black, he had the Bauhaus logo hand-drawn across the front of his shirt in white paint. His layers of Halloween greasepaint makeup couldn't hide the fact that he had coke-bottle glasses and enough acne to populate decades' worth of Stridex commercials.

The thing is, he thought to himself defiantly, he couldn't even remember why the teacher sent him here. Ever since "the metamorphosis," as he labeled his wardrobe change, some teachers just seemed to want to send him to the office to break his spirit. Last week, the gym teacher even called him "freak-boy."

When the guidance counselor heard this, she hit the ceiling, demanding that the teacher get fired. However, the principal reminded her that this was the football coach she was talking about—his job had meaning, unlike someone he wouldn't name out loud.

Next to Poe was a pretty girl. He knew he'd seen her before, but she looked different. Did she always look this beautiful?

"So, what are you in for?" he asked her in his best imitation of an acne-scarred Humphrey Bogart.

"Murder," she deadpanned, trying to sound like Brando.

Poe laughed, which wasn't necessarily a good thing for him, as it was against the rules that came with his uniform. But he liked girls with a sense of humor, or at least he thought he did. "I like you. Do you want to be my Lenore?" he blurted out before he could control the impulse.

Damn. He had come on too strong. He'd been afraid he would do that. He always did. Sensing Sam's immediate lack of interest, he gave up before he stuck his foot in his mouth again. "Really, what are you in for?"

"Fucked if I—" Finally, the Principal poked his head out of his inner office. Just Poe's luck. She had continued talking to him even after he'd made a fool of himself. In his world, that never happened.

"Alright little Miss Potty Mouth, get your buns in here!" the principal boomed, only a half-step out of his sanctuary, eyeing Poe.

"—know," she finished. She grabbed her Trapper Keeper off the floor next to her chair and followed the principal into the abyss.

Inside his office, the principals' walls were covered with dozens of paddles, many with holes drilled into them to reduce wind resistance. Besides these relics of a bygone era, the room looked like any other generic wood-paneled office.

"Missy, you're just lucky I can't use any of these anymore," he barked while nodding his head towards the artillery. "By God, I would love to give you what for."

The principal stopped, remembering the meeting he'd had to attend about how to speak to teenage girls in this newly liberated age.

"Damn school board won't even let me wash out your mouth with soap. Bleeding heart commie long hairs. Instead, you're going to be here all Saturday to think about what you've done." He sure had liked it when he could spank them.

Rocking gently back and forth like a teenybopper at her first sock-hop, Sam hummed.

Participation Trophy

"Well, do you have anything to say for yourself, little girl?" he boomed.

Troy's Funeral

The church they held the two all-stars' funerals in was undeniably Catholic. But, with its fluorescent lights and plastic statues, it looked like it was set-dressed by Stanley Kubrick.

The mourners wrote off their mental images of big Catholic cathedrals as something only in movies where hunchbacks swung and rang the bells. This church had a button that let out a chime when pressed, a digital tone that could be heard for blocks around.

The priest stood at a bright white plastic altar. Rail thin, he commanded the stage like a Shakespearean actor, which he might have been, if his mother had not found the package to him postmarked from an undisclosed address in Amsterdam.

Shit, time to start—break a leg, the priest thought. "Troy . . . Troy . . ." The words stuck in his throat as he tried to swallow the big lie he was about to say before the Almighty, His flock, and all the paying customers. "Troy . . . was a good boy."

Looking down at the body in the casket, all he thought was, what a waste.

John's Room Again

John and Sam sat around playing their ever-popular game of not talking. "See, I told you something like this was going to happen," John said, losing.

"See, I told you something like this would happen," Sam parroted back.

"Anyway, you said if I skipped! I didn't skip. Everyone is acting like the world is ending because I dropped an f-bomb in class. You should have heard him chewing out my ass." She paused, putting the finger on the humor in her words. "You wouldn't believe the other things he wanted to do to it, either!

"Anyway, it's one Saturday in the library, haven't you seen The Breakfast Club? Maybe if I play my cards right, I can get knocked up by Judd Nelson in the teen-pregnancy section."

"Sure . . . have fun with that," John lamely retorted in the face of the irony and sarcasm that radiated off Sam like a mushroom cloud.

Perfectly aping the principal. "Missy, you're lucky the school board won't let me make you stand on rocks anymore, while I fuck you up the ass, to prove that you're not a witch!" Her voice went back to her own, though cold and empty. "You're just lucky that we don't rip cocks off and flush them down the toilet—at least not in this institution."

John stared back at her, but the cloud of self-induced haziness was quickly making him forget the oddness of her statement. "That was a pretty good imitation. All you needed was a red nose and a bottle of Red Label in your desk."

Sam remembered the time in second grade when John had bloodied Jared's nose for what he said to her, of course that was immediately before he was ganged up on by all the future jock-os. She wanted John back—the sweet one. The one who would do anything for her. Or potentially to her. Her mind wandered while John sat there staring at nothing at all.

He wasn't a lost cause—not yet, at least.

She certainly wouldn't sit in perpetual bored silence with anybody else. From beside her, she picked up the copy of Seventeen that she had brought with her.

Protection

John and Sam laid kissing on his bed. In the background, some British synth band whose name John couldn't remember droned on and on.

Sam started kissing John's neck, first one side, then the other. His head rolled back in the pure warm moment. The desire for this had been building for quite some time. She had said so herself before she'd started kissing him. Right?

As his head sunk back into his sci-fi-themed pillow, why did it hurt so much? A sudden gush of blood arced in the air. John airlessly screamed, unable to make a sound from his torn throat.

Sam's head rose with the flesh of his neck hanging out of her mouth, a mouth that was full of razor-sharp teeth.

As she spoke, a large strip of skin fell out of her mouth. "What's wrong? Were we not ready for this? I have protection!" she said, flopping the dark leather book down on the bed next to him.

John woke up screaming, noticing he was alone in his bed. From the feel of it, he was sure there was nobody in the entire house.

It was late, and the music from his dream was playing on the stereo. He looked around for the joint he was smoking, found his ashtray, and put it out.

It wasn't the first time he'd had a sexy dream, though it was the first in a while that it had been Sam in the lead role. And it was definitely the first time it ended with blood gushing out of his neck.

Spraying Lysol to cover up the smell of the weed, he looked uncomfortably down at his jeans. Touching them, he brought his hand to eye-level, a look of disappointment on his face.

Ally, Molly, Judd, Anthony, and Emilio

Sam had never realized it before, but their library was a dead ringer for the one in a particular John Hughes movie. This realization filled her heart with unexpected joy when she walked in ten minutes before detention began. Maybe if someone were holding, she would get stoned and dance on the railing of the second floor in a montage sequence.

Where was John when you needed him?

After the seats started filling, Sam was pretty sure nobody was getting wasted today. She sat where Ally would have been. Where Judd would be was a jock. Then where Emilio would be was a jock. Where Anthony would be was—surprise, surprise—another jock. However, where Molly would be . . . one of the Tiffanies. For fuck's sake, where's the nerd and the burn-out?

Fuck Hollywood, she thought. Nothing but goddamn lies.

Looking at her reflection in the polished wood of the huge table, Sam checked on the makeup she hoped was hiding how pale she'd become. Between that and the dress she was wearing, the first one in as long as she could remember, she thought her mom might even admit she did seem just a little bit like a real life, living and breathing "girl." If her mom was ever around.

Sitting alone, and a little vexed that her pubescent fantasy had fallen on its ass, she became even more annoyed when she saw both Poe and another jock arrive. Fuck this! she said to herself before doing a dead-on faceplant onto the tabletop.

Even though Poe eyed Sam first, the jock sat next to her and Poe reluctantly sat on the other side of the table.

"What brings a bad girl like you to a place like—" Poe started, but the jock looked at him, cutting off another misguided attempt.

Looking her up and down like a piece of meat, the jock interrupted, "Is this freak bothering you?"

Sam mocked a blush, but still looked the wrong side of death. Her pallid complexion made Poe look like George Hamilton.

"Yeah, he is, but it's okay." Behind her back, the jock menaced Poe, who flinched, despite being several feet away.

"Are you new here? I haven't seen you around before. Here, I mean, school." The jock slowly put together the fragments of his monosyllabic pick-up skills. "Not the library, is what I'm sayin'."

Sam started in with the wise-ass routine. "We've lived in the same town forever." Her initial smarminess gave way to blatant flirtation. "Why haven't you ever noticed?"

The jock tried to get a better look at her, apparently not even listening. "Whatchu doing after this?"

Underneath the table, out of sight of her two suitors, Sam's hand balled into a fist.

"Nothing. You?"

Halfway through detention, Sam and the jock slipped out of the library, and after a few minutes of looking, they found themselves in the locker room. So, this is what the boys' locker room looks like, Sam thought. She'd pictured something even grosser, but it still had a certain boy smell that was far from pleasant.

Dispensing with the small talk, the jock went straight for her neck and started kissing it, oblivious to the look of disgust on her face. Soon, the disgusted look melted.

" . . . So, is this happening . . . ?" he asked, taking off his shirt. He flexed for himself in the mirror behind Sam's head, a look of I'd fuck me crossing his face.

What a good gentleman, she thought. No rape vibes, at least not yet. Well, not many.

He stepped back and dropped his jeans and underwear in one fell swoop.

Completely nude, the jock stood before her like an idol waiting to be worshiped. This was the first time Sam had seen a real-live naked man.

From her peripheral vision, she saw her fist swing, connect, and knock him down. Before she realized what she was doing, she found herself standing above him like a wolf ready to kill its prey. She reached down between his legs and an effeminate scream echoed off the tiles.

Hallway Conversation

As they walked down the hall, John was trying his hardest not to notice that Sam was wearing a look straight out of a gothic Debbie Gibson video, had there been such a thing. He was also trying not to think of the dreams he'd been having about her.

When he saw Sarah walking the other way, his focus shifted. "I'll be right back, see you in class," he told Sam as he half-jogged off. From the look on her face, he might as well have said, "I'm going to have a word with this Hitler fellow for a moment!"

"Sure thing, pal," Sam told the invisible outline of where John had been just a moment before.

"Everything okay?" John asked, slipping up behind Sarah with such ghost-like silence that it made her jump. It took her a second to recognize him. It had been weeks since anyone had dared talk to her in the halls, let alone Kevin's brother.

A weary smile crossed her face. "Yeah, haven't been getting enough sleep. I've been getting pervy ... um ... well, pervier calls this last week. Some of them have been threatening. It's almost worse than when ..."

John, still a few words behind, cut in. He could blame the half-smoked bag of weed, but if he was honest with himself, women always made him feel like he'd skipped a page or two in a book. "Calls? Who's calling you?"

"Yeah, they haven't stopped since the day ... the day after. Everyone around here has been treating me like the Whore of Babylon, or a murderer, or both."

A glimmer of anger broke through John's fatigue.

"It would be one thing if I got blasted on PBR and blew the starting lineup; that, everyone would be fine with. One of the cheerleaders does that about once a week. A story goes around that you spread your legs for the entire team, you're a slut, even if it didn't happen."

John looked at her like he was still processing the word "calls." This conversation was just a bit over his reading level. The thought that maybe it hadn't happened the way it'd been relayed to him a million times already had never crossed his mind.

"Forget it. This entire year has felt like someone tipped over the first domino and I've been trying to keep all the other ones upright." She paused, feeling embittered. "The past month has felt like years."

"Yeah, I get you . . . I think."

Awkward silence. John was good at awkward silence. He could get a trophy if they decided to make it a school-sponsored extracurricular. Maybe even had a chance at all-national.

Without saying goodbye, Sarah went on to class.

Health Class Blues

Bartleby was talking to the class. It was just a dull hum of catchphrases about Jesus, why not to do drugs, and his favorite topic since he'd broached the subject last week—Satan, Satan, Satan! Methinks he doth protest too much! Sam pictured him coming home, switching to sneakers, Mr. Rogers style, before slipping into his cardigan of human skin.

"So, what did you have to say to—" Sam managed to whisper low enough that it went under Bartleby's radar.

John cut her off before she could get out the pitchfork she had been sharpening in her mind. "Nothing. She just looked bad, so I had to—"

Sam looked down at her hands, pissed about the entire situation. Why was it so vital for him to talk to

Sarah? She was the one who was driving them apart, at least that's what she felt in her dreams.

"She always looks bad."

"Why? I mean, why this? You still haven't explained to me why you have to be so mean to her," John responded as Sarah's knight in dorky, weed-scented armor.

Sam started Hulking out—well if the Incredible Hulk had been an about five foot three, ninety-pound freshman. "After what she did to your—"

"Were you there? Do you know what happened? Because if you were, I'd have some big questions to ask." A look of hurt spread across his face.

"Well, all I'm saying is maybe she should be the one buying the farm around here," Sam mumbled feebly.

"That's not funny. A bunch of kids have been dying. It's fucking weird." The word "fuck" slid off his tongue in a register that only dogs could hear.

"Nah, suicide amongst popular kids is like the common cold; one kid gets it, and the rest start picking it up from the doorknobs," she added with a smirk.

"Troy, okay. But suicide by diving headfirst into a fire? Suicide by pulling off your penis and bleeding out in the locker room?"

"It's possible!" Sam made an exaggerated act of choking herself while ripping off an imaginary object from below her waist, and then made a sound like a wet paper towel getting pulled off a linoleum floor. The thought made her whisper a hysterical giggle.

This high-school eugenics talk was a tad out of place for their well-established pool of interests. "What's with this attitude?" John asked. "Nobody should be dying around here. We're in 10th grade for fu—" The tone of his voice went from quiet to a whisper. "—Christ's sake." he checked to see if

Bartleby heard him, which would have made things worse.

Impatience

Again, John's lips pressed against hers. The dead skunk smell of pot filled her nose. When she opened her eyes, John was already up from the bed and walking upstairs.

Sarah sat next to Sam in bed. "You know you're losing him, right? You know what you have to do. What's taking you so fucking long? Are you a chicken or what?" Sarah handed Sam a knife.

In her hand, it felt oddly gelatinous, but she woke up before she could see why it had been wet and warm to her.

Bedroom Doctrine

John laid in bed half asleep, absently turning through one of the Hustlers. A redhead, a blonde, an Asian girl, another blonde, the next one a younger version of Helen. She was posed seductively in an even tinier version of her already revealing waitress uniform. Not believing his eyes, he continued to flip. All the way to the middle, it was nothing but pictures of her. When he finally unfolded the centerfold, it was Helen in a WWII pin-up pose.

From within the centerfold, Helen started striking other poses, like she was auditioning for a Whitesnake video. She blew kisses to unseen people behind the camera, she spanked herself and gave a little oh no, I've been bad look as she covered her mouth in surprise.

She stopped and stared longingly at John from the other side of the paper. "I saw you looking at me," she said to him in her best Marilyn Monroe. "So, what did you have on your mind, sweetheart?" she said, arching her arms forward to squeeze her breasts together.

John looked down at the tiny waitress, his mouth slightly parted in disbelief like he'd just seen a ghost. Or was a nearly nude centerfold model really talking to him from inside a magazine?

Helen glanced around around the inside of the photo set, over-pantomiming an I'm uncomfortable in here look, acting claustrophobic inside the walls of the page. Then a look of I have an idea! crossed her face and she approached the front of the set. Reaching towards the camera her hand slipped through, full-sized, from inside the page.

"Ahh . . . that's the stuff." She giggled and gave John a seductive wink.

Participation Trophy

This twenty-something version of Helen started pulling herself out of the magazine, first her hands, then her head. She widened the edges of the page as if they were elastic. In short order, she had her entire torso out of the magazine. The elasticity seemed to have given as much as it could. Her pin-up's hips were just a little too wide to get out of the page.

"Can I get a hand here?" she asked, but then she noticed she was emerging directly out of the top of John's lap. "Oh!" She giggled. "No dear, I guess you're in no position to do that!"

Helen started to wriggle her hips from side to side and finally freed herself from the page. Sitting on John's lap, she pulled her legs out from the magazine like a synchronized swimmer in an old movie and crossed them with a little kick.

"Where was I . . ." She laughed again and gave him Betty Boop eyes. She kicked the magazine to the ground. "Oh, that's right." She started over again, looking off into the distance like she was reading a cue card. "I've seen the way you've been looking at me."

Helen stroked John's chest seductively, making cartoon-kissy faces at him. The words came out of her mouth like dialogue out of a daytime soap. "I could just eat you like a slice of yummy . . . cheese pizza."

The age difference made John feel uncomfortable, even though Helen appeared to be younger than when he saw her at Joe's. It was one thing to fantasize about something. It was another thing entirely to find your fantasy literally on your lap.

"I find boys like you so . . . delicioso," she cooed at him.

Her words were stilted and almost purposefully bad in their delivery, though it wasn't like Orson Welles ever wrote porno scripts. Well, not porno that John had watched. But the way she was talking to him was making him more uncomfortable than turned on.

Helen repositioned herself so she was straddling John. She lowered her head and her long wavy brown hair covered her face. When she looked back up, it was now Sam's face on Helen's body. John's hand instinctively went to his throat, remembering the dream from a few days ago. Using Helen's voice, Sam said, "Don't you want me, sweets?"

Sam, in her own body but dressed in the waitress' outfit, grabbed John by the collar and started kissing him like a wolf in a Tex Avery cartoon. Pulling back, but not forcefully enough to change the situation in the least, he moved his head to the side while she continued to kiss the corner of his mouth, and then his cheek, and then his neck.

"Sam, what are you doing?" John looked embarassed, and then his eyes rolled backwards before his head fell back with a skull-cracking thud.

With John unconscious, Sam got up and went

behind his bed to the hole of mystery. For a moment, she fumbled around, pulling out dirty magazines and tossing them over her shoulder behind her. It wasn't an extensive collection, but Larry Flynt would have been proud.

Finally, she pulled out the book. Opening it up to the middle, Sam found what remained of the weed in a small bag. She picked it up with her index finger and thumb, as if it were something dirty she'd found in the middle of the street, and tossed it to the side.

Sam kissed her hand and planted it on the top of John's head.. This had been fun, but there would be more time for that later. She put the book under her arm and made a hasty retreat.

Sam's Room Revisited

In the center of Sam's pale pink bedspread sat Poe. He looked confused and out of place. Anybody with eyes could spot that this was the first time he'd been in a girl's room.

The room wasn't what he'd been expecting. Still, most of his mental images of women's places came from the Victorian Gothics he'd been checking out obsessively from the library for the past several months.

Definitely fewer candles than he pictured.

Feeling helpless, he started trying to fill the air he felt he was drowning in. This was a dangerous game, talking to a girl. He wasn't good at it, but he tried anyway.

"I knew that you were just using Brad to make me jealous." He laughed nervously.

Standing in the middle of the room, Sam looked down at him, giving him a look that clearly showed she didn't know what the fuck he was talking about.

She pulled out a candle from her desk drawer, and Poe felt a little vindicated. Aha, at least there is one thing I was expecting, he thought, and this gave him enough courage to continue.

"You know, when you went off with Brad the other day during detention, it was just to get my attention, right?" His words hung. It felt like all the air had been sucked out of the room.

Sam's face conveyed an "oh" moment that betrayed that she wasn't even aware of the jock's name until now. Frankly, she wasn't entirely sure she knew the name of the boy on her bed, or 99.9% of the kids in her class for that matter, even though they had inhabited the same schools for over a decade.

Participation Trophy

Poe sprayed Binaca in his mouth. He started in expectantly; 10% Don Juan, 90% never been kissed.

"So, why did you invite me over? "

Sam looked at Poe seductively. Leaning over him, she dodged his puckered lips at the last minute, reached behind one of her pillows, and pulled out the book.

𝒟ead, 𝒟ead, 𝒟ead to me, 𝒟ead, 𝒟ead

The two remaining Tiffanies stood in the hallway looking at the school newspaper. The front page had a shot of the entire football team smiling for the camera, with the Tiffanies crouching below, the middle Tiff doing the splits in the front. The headline read "Football Season Over."

The Tiffany on the left pulled out a Magic Marker and started X-ing out faces. "Dead, dead, dead to me, dead, dead. Ugh, that thing," she said pointing at the heavy-set girl with braces in the front row. Being the daughter of the cheer coach shouldn't give you a pass. "Dead, dead, and I think I heard that she transferred to Lincoln, that little . . .

"Fuck, I even think the fucking dork who took

the picture went missing the other day. You know, these geeks are disappearing because they don't have the guts to die like the popular kids. They're probably pumping quarters into Donkey Kong somewhere, fucking losers."

With this, she gave a little sigh and once again swallowed her emotions, forcing them down into the already overcrowded pit in her stomach. One day she would unload that pit onto her therapist, the same way she discharged her lunch in the bathroom.

Sam and Poe walked down the hall. Dressed head to toe in black, Sam looked like a teenage fashion queen by way of Elvira. Poe, seemingly led by an invisible leash, walked a few paces behind. They passed by John as if he didn't even exist.

Joe's Pizza

John sat alone in the pizza place, fiddling with his straw. When Helen came up from behind, he flinched ever so slightly, partially because he had forgotten that he'd already ordered, and partially because of the half-remembered dream from the other night.

"What's wrong, sweets?" she asked with her glossy Dianetics smile, but apparently actually concerned about the kid. "You seem down in the dumps. Where's your little friend?"

John shrugged his shoulders like a man who'd been in a bar all night over a woman. He was a fedora and a cigarette away from asking her to "play it again." Though wasn't that really a question for Sam? Helen put a soggy paper plate down in front of him.

Participation Trophy

"Well, you know what? The 'za's on me, honey." Her good deed for the day. Not that she would have to pay for it—she had been freely stealing from Joe for years, ever since she found out about his little proclivity. Turns out Joe was even pervier than he looked.

John faked a smile as she walked away. He was too frightened by what had happened the other night to check out her ass. Not that he needed to; over the last couple weeks he had stared at it so often that he could have picked it out of a police lineup.

The restaurant doors flung open, sending the bell clanging across the floor. John had his back to the commotion. He didn't even turn around to look, hardly caring and not taking notice until he heard the intruder yelling at Joe in the kitchen.

". . . my DAUGHTER, MAN! What kind of sick fuck are you?? You're probably the one who's offing all the other kids, too, you FUCKING

PERVERT!"

Gunshots rang out, and John dove low in the booth as the shooter ran out the door and tires squealed.

John wasted no time getting the fuck out of Dodge.

John ran down train tracks, the embankments infinitely more covered in Satanic graffiti than before. He saw some goth kids spray-painting huge letters. Was that Eric and one of the other missing kids?

Couldn't be them, though. These two kids looked like they were waiting for The Cult to come to town.

In his panic, he continued running without much regard for what they were doing. Not paying attention, he didn't register that they were writing "John & Helen 4-Ever" with little hearts and arrows cutely decorating it.

Kevin

Kevin sat in his bed, looking down at the revolver in his hand. Low in the background, Joy Division played.

Sarah sat next to him. On his other side, the book laid open. Kevin couldn't believe what he was hearing. He had known the rumors weren't true, but the way Sarah wanted to fix the situation was making his head spin and stomach hurt.

"You know what we should do to them," Sarah said in a cool, low voice. "There's only one way to make this right. Those little bitches should burn, too. I don't know who started the rumor, but they should all pay."

His head was swarming with images of what she wanted him to do. He couldn't take it. Suddenly, he thought of a way to let them out.

Sarah wasn't mad at him for what he did then, just disappointed.

Dorks, Dweebs and Geeks

John stood in front of the door to Sam's bedroom. There was a strange silence in the air. It felt creepy—like nobody was on the other side. He thought for a moment that she might not be there. John hadn't seen her at school that day. He banged on the door again.

After what felt like an eternity, the door swung open, and Poe stood inside, a silent and vacant Renfield to Sam's Dracula. Lying in bed on her stomach, she flipped through the book, her legs crossed in the air, swaying back and forth. She pretended to be engrossed in her reading material.

"You . . . you . . . you wouldn't believe what just happened at the pizza place!" he stammered out.

Sam gave him the disappointed look of someone who has spent hours preparing for a surprise party where the birthday boy comes in and starts eating the chips and commenting on the streamers.

Annoyed, Sam looked to Poe, who walked over from behind the door and slid a knife right into John's spine.

John collapsed like a marionette that had its strings cut in one quick snip.

From the floor, John looked up at Sam as the edges of his vision started to blur. A ringing filled his ears. Her voice began to filter through the gauze of pain.

"It was always supposed to be us, you know? But you're too fucking oblivious to what's in front of you." With this, Sam's shoe landed on his face. John felt the small bones inside his nose breaking. Her words hurt, but not as much as her foot.

Participation Trophy

John swam in the darkness. If this was death, he thought, maybe death wasn't so bad.

The room John woke up in looked like it hadn't been inhabited for many years before that night. It was claustrophobic and dirty, barely fitting the dozen or so missing dorks, dweebs, and geeks who stood around a circle painted on the floor with blood. Their faces were caked with clown-white makeup, crudely drawn logos for different goth and metal bands adorned their shirts.

In the center of the bloody circle, John had been laid down on his back, stripped to his tighty-whities. Paralyzed, for a moment he closed his eyes trying to will his arm to move, but he soon realized that trying to pull a Jedi mind trick wasn't going to work.

Mr. Bartleby, Helen, and Sarah stood behind a ramshackle altar. The book in hand, Bartleby started reading aloud.

John vaguely recognized the words as the same ones that had come out of Sam's mouth only a few weeks ago. That felt like forever ago to him as he trembled in a pool of his own blood, his white underwear slowly becoming pink.

The unhealthy lime-green light radiated from behind Bartleby as he continued to chant.

All the kids intently watched John as they waited for something, anything, to happen. From some unseen location, Sam emerged. Bending down, she started kissing him and touching his cheek.

"This isn't goodbye," she said. "They promised me."

Bartleby, Helen, Sarah, Sam, and the circle of painted misfits all waited expectantly for whatever the payoff was going to be after all this build-up.

Metaphorical crickets chirped.

Sam lost this silence game. "Is that it? No huge

crack with Beelzebub flying out? No Devil? No . . . no nothing? You said that he would love me, that he would be with me forever!"

"These things don't always turn out the way anybody wants them to, hon." Helen said to Sam. Then Mr. Bartleby and Helen shrugged, hooked their arms and walked away. With a smile, Sarah curtsied. "Thanks for doing the dirty work, bitch!" Casually picking up the book from the altar, she followed the other two. One happy little cult.

Their followers began to leave in no particular hurry, and Sam watched the life slowly leave John's body. Unceremoniously, he let go of his last breath, and Sam was alone.

For a romantic second, Sam thought about Julieting her way after him. The next, she thought that, if this were one of her comics, this is where he would start breathing again.

www.ingramcontent.com/pod-product-compliance
Lightning Source LLC
LaVergne TN
LVHW031613060526
838201LV00065B/4826